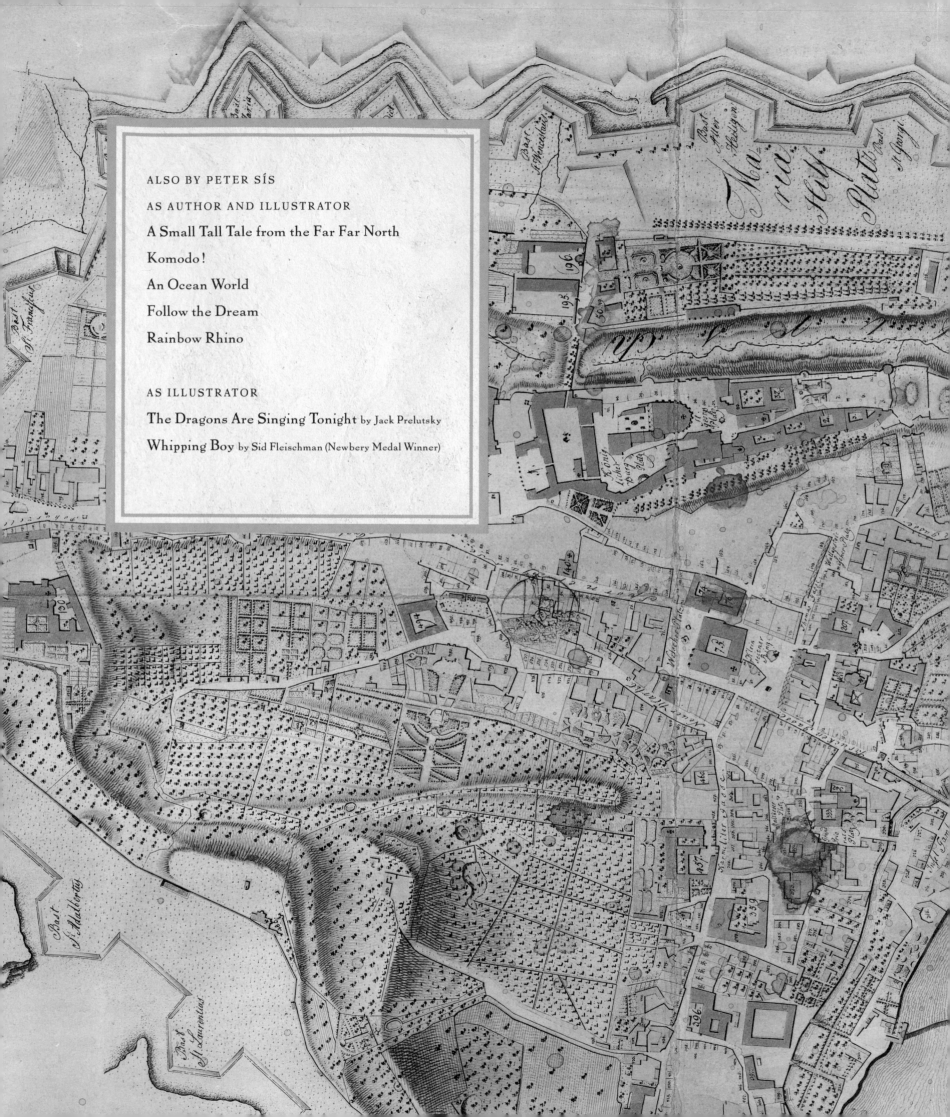

ALSO BY PETER SÍS

AS AUTHOR AND ILLUSTRATOR

A Small Tall Tale from the Far Far North

Komodo!

An Ocean World

Follow the Dream

Rainbow Rhino

AS ILLUSTRATOR

The Dragons Are Singing Tonight by Jack Prelutsky

Whipping Boy by Sid Fleischman (Newbery Medal Winner)

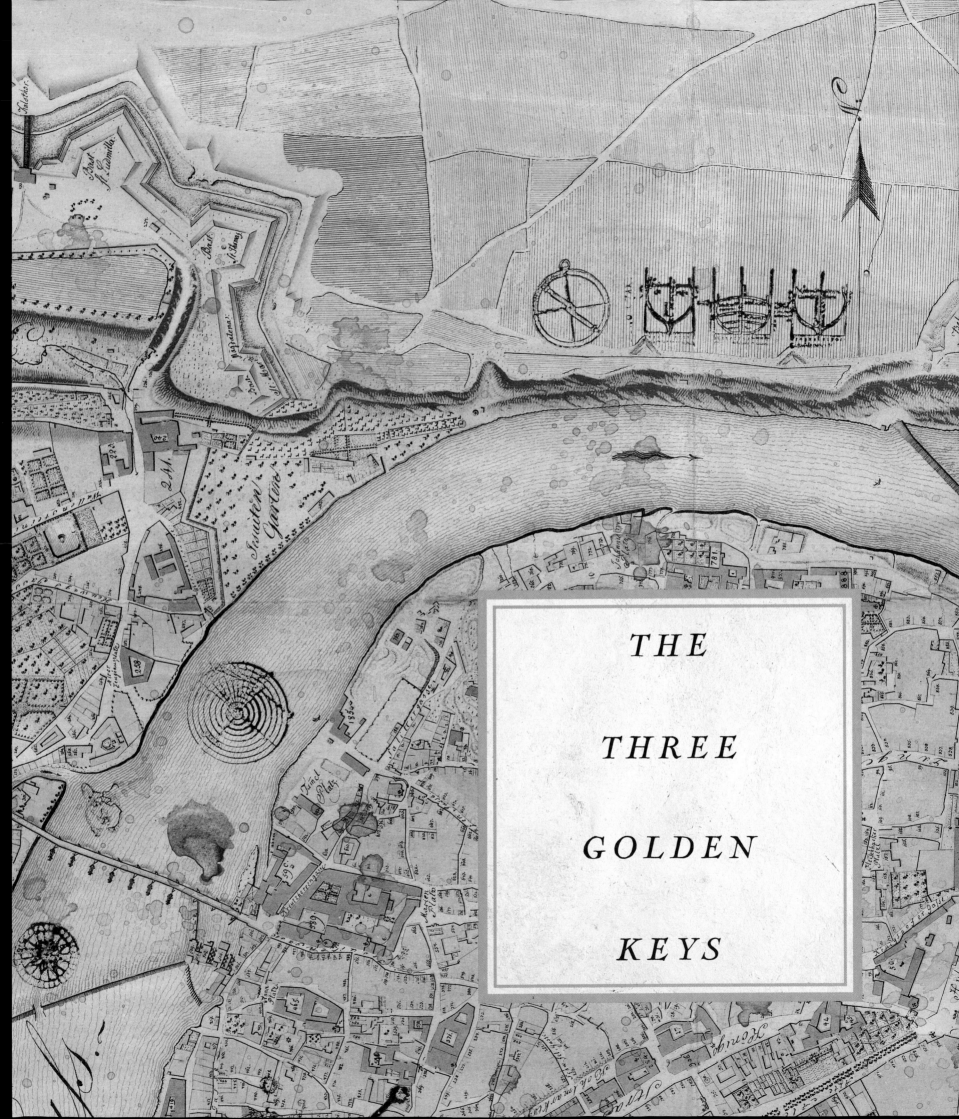

THE

THREE

GOLDEN

KEYS

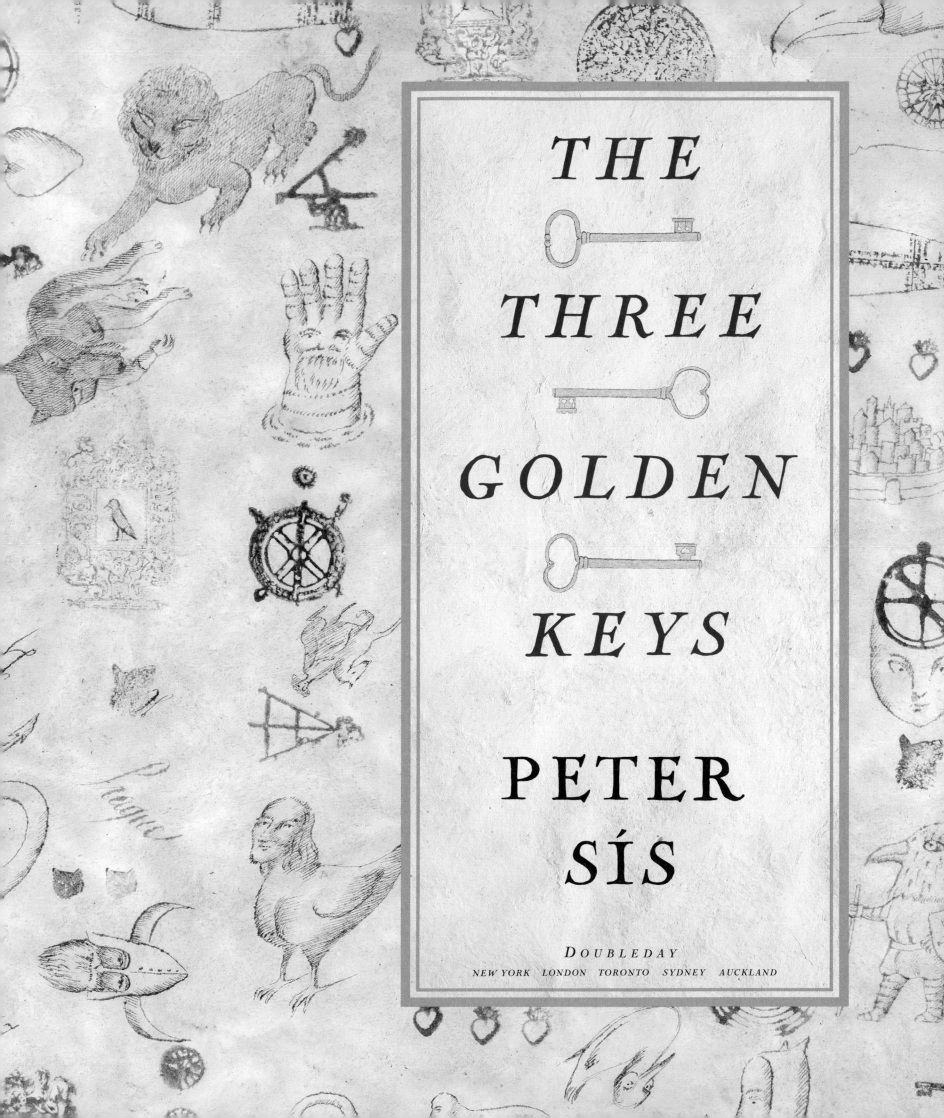

THE
THREE
GOLDEN
KEYS

PETER
SÍS

DOUBLEDAY

NEW YORK LONDON TORONTO SYDNEY AUCKLAND

PUBLISHED BY DOUBLEDAY
a division of Bantam Doubleday Dell Publishing Group, Inc.
1540 Broadway, New York, New York 10036

DOUBLEDAY and the portrayal of an anchor with a dolphin
are trademarks of Doubleday, a division of
Bantam Doubleday Dell Publishing Group, Inc.

Book design by Marysarah Quinn

Library of Congress Cataloging-in-Publication Data
Sís, Peter.
The three golden keys / Peter Sís. — 1st ed.
p. cm.
Summary: Led by a cat on a magical journey through Prague, a man
encounters some of the city's landmarks and three traditional Czech
fairy tales while trying to find the keys to his childhood home.
[1. Fairy tales. 2. Prague (Czech Republic)—Fiction.]
I. Title.
PZ7.S362Th   1994
[E]—dc20   94-6743
                                                        CIP
                                                        AC

ISBN 0-385-47292-7

Copyright © 1994 by Peter Sís
All Rights Reserved
Printed in Italy
November 1994

3 5 7 9 10 8 6 4 2

Thank you for a dream J.O.!

NEW YORK
1994

My Dear Madeleine,

Sweet little round daughter with beautiful eyes and constant smile.
By the time you can make sense of this note it will be the 21st century.
You were born in New York, in the New World, and surely you will be wondering
one day where your father came from. This book is to explain just that.
You might never speak Czech. You may prefer other parts of this beautiful
planet – blue seas, green islands, bustling metropolises. You are free.
However, one day you will enter Prague, the place I grew up, in your silent
slippers soft as cat's paws, and you will look for the keys. Maybe.
If you find the keys, unlock the mystery of Prague very, very slowly. I could
give you dates, I could give you history, but only you will decide if you
want to know. You might find some of my lost marbles I played with.
You will hear the same bells I listened to in my childhood. Prague
is a magic place if you take time! Rainer Maria Rilke wrote:

"I know my little mother Prague to her very heart, to her very heart...
the heart always keeps the deepest secrets, and there are many
secrets in these old houses."

By the way, don't be afraid of the old black cats... they might just be
hobgoblins in cat's clothing...

Kiss Kiss

PETER

TO SHAYE ARCHEART

Madeleine . . .

A wild and turbulent storm took control of my hot-air balloon
and sent me far off course.

When the storm finally calmed, I found myself floating toward
the spires of a big city.

I did not have time to wonder about the city, as my balloon was rapidly losing air.

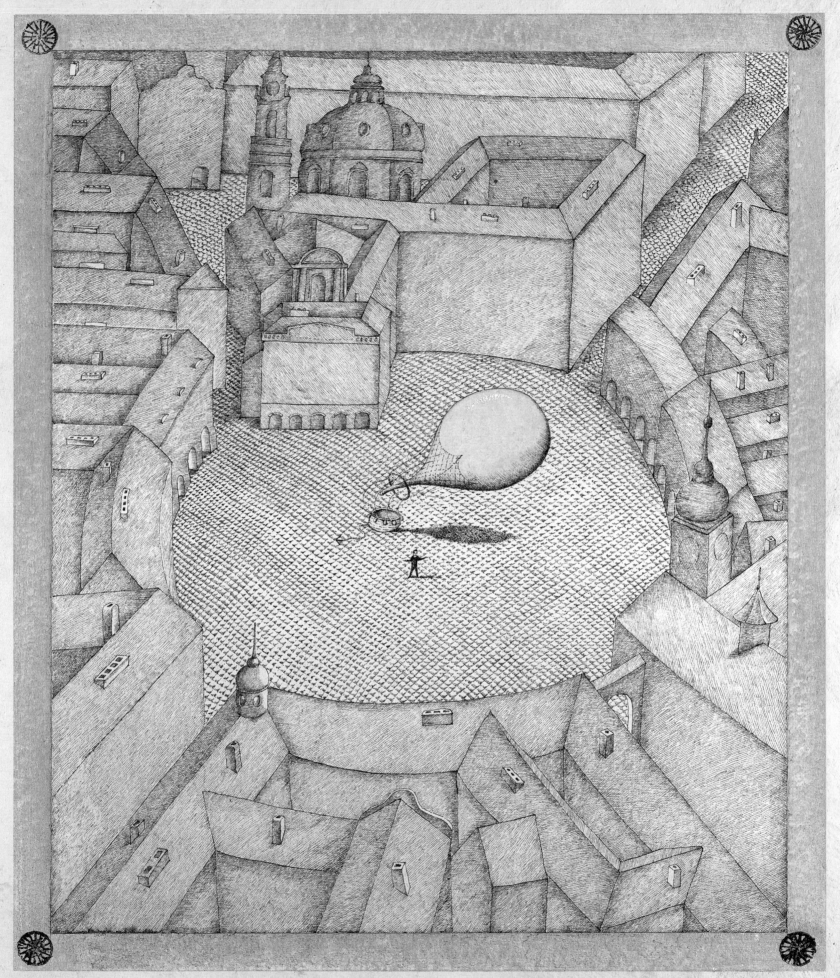

I was lucky to land unharmed on a deserted square.
I quickly got out of the gondola.

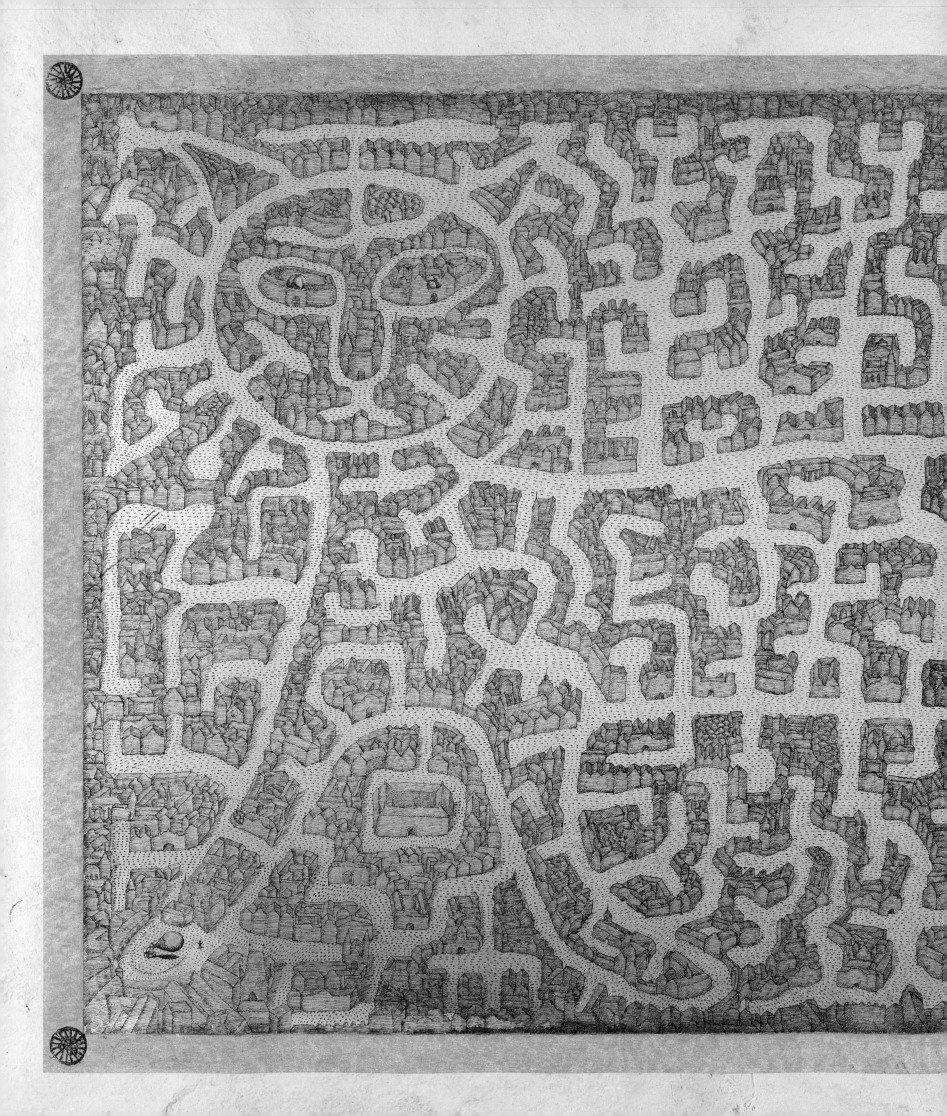

There was nobody anywhere. But, all of a sudden, everything around me reminded me of my childhood . . . Could it be that the storm had taken me all the way back to Prague, where I grew up? Would I still remember the way through the twisting streets to my family house?

Our family house . . . Here it was, with all its memories. Is anybody home?
There are three rusty padlocks on the door. Three padlocks I have no keys to . . .

I have to get the keys. But there is nobody around . . . Then, out of nowhere,
comes our black cat. Can it really be my cat after all these years? Somehow,
I know she wants me to follow her.

I follow my cat through the winter streets of my childhood—all those games, sledding on the first snow with the tips of my ears freezing, tea with lemon, the stove in the dark—two eyes of fire . . .

The cat waits for me as I wander the empty streets filled with December memories—my sister's birthday, Saint Nicholas with his angel and his devil. "Presents for the good children, coal for the bad!" Christmas-time with carp in the bathtub, family visits, and a magical tree.

I follow my cat for a long time. Every house, every window, every cobblestone brings back some memory. The signs on the old buildings tell of good times and bad. We are heading toward the castle . . .

Before we reach the castle, the cat turns to the library,
another place I loved to visit as a child . . .

The door is open . . . and everything is as it used to be . . .
The library is deserted . . . and quiet.

There is a shift in the wall of books ahead of me . . .

The librarian magically emerges from the wall. I have seen him before
in some old painting. He moves toward me, holding a scroll.

Other characters
emerge from the
rows of books,
silently and
majestically. The
librarian unrolls
the scroll—there
is a golden key
attached to it.
He gives it
to me . . .

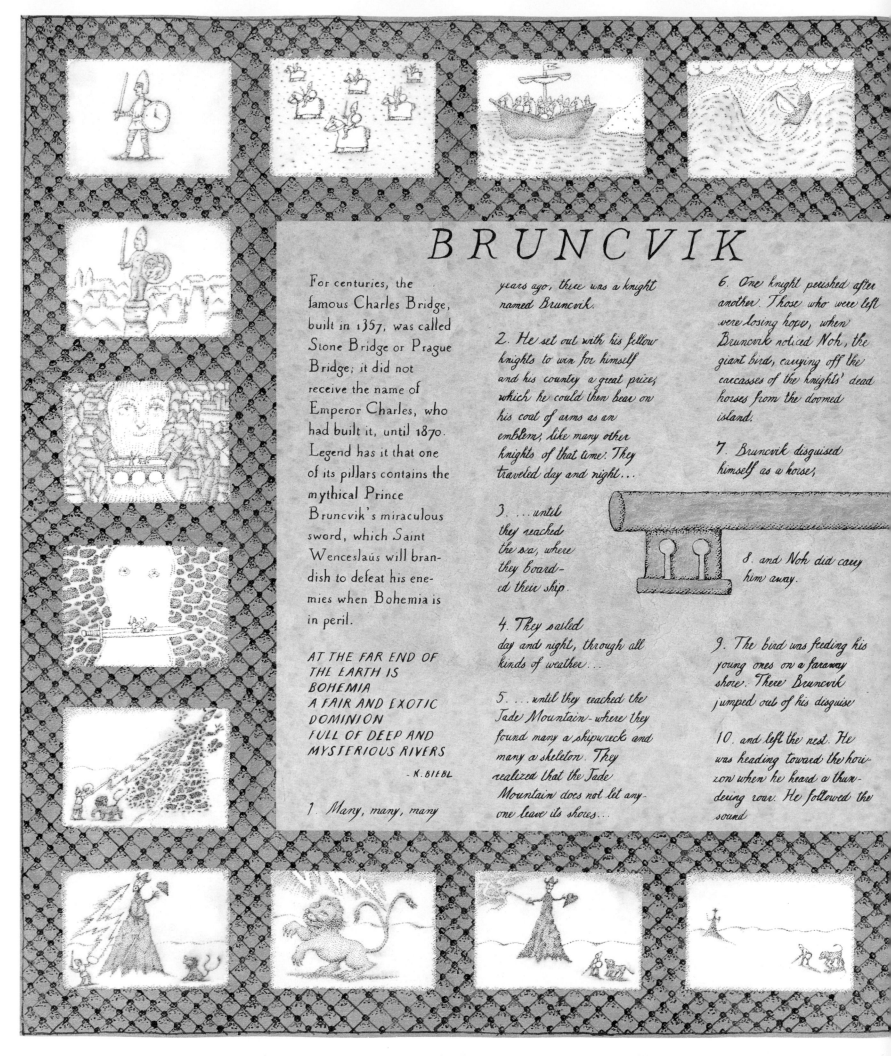

BRUNCVIK

For centuries, the famous Charles Bridge, built in 1357, was called Stone Bridge or Prague Bridge; it did not receive the name of Emperor Charles, who had built it, until 1870. Legend has it that one of its pillars contains the mythical Prince Bruncvik's miraculous sword, which Saint Wenceslaus will brandish to defeat his enemies when Bohemia is in peril.

AT THE FAR END OF
THE EARTH IS
BOHEMIA
A FAIR AND EXOTIC
DOMINION
FULL OF DEEP AND
MYSTERIOUS RIVERS
— K. BIEBL

1. Many, many, many years ago, there was a knight named Bruncvik.

2. He set out with his fellow knights to win for himself and his country a great prize, which he could then bear on his coat of arms as an emblem, like many other knights of that time. They traveled day and night...

3. ...until they reached the sea, where they boarded their ship.

4. They sailed day and night, through all kinds of weather...

5. ...until they reached the Jade Mountain—where they found many a shipwreck and many a skeleton. They realized that the Jade Mountain does not let anyone leave its shores...

6. One knight perished after another. Those who were left were losing hope, when Bruncvik noticed Noh, the giant bird, carrying off the carcasses of the knights' dead horses from the doomed island.

7. Bruncvik disguised himself as a horse,

8. and Noh did carry him away.

9. The bird was feeding his young ones on a faraway shore. There Bruncvik jumped out of his disguise

10. and left the nest. He was heading toward the horizon when he heard a thundering roar. He followed the sound

I read the story on the ancient scroll. It is a story from my childhood.

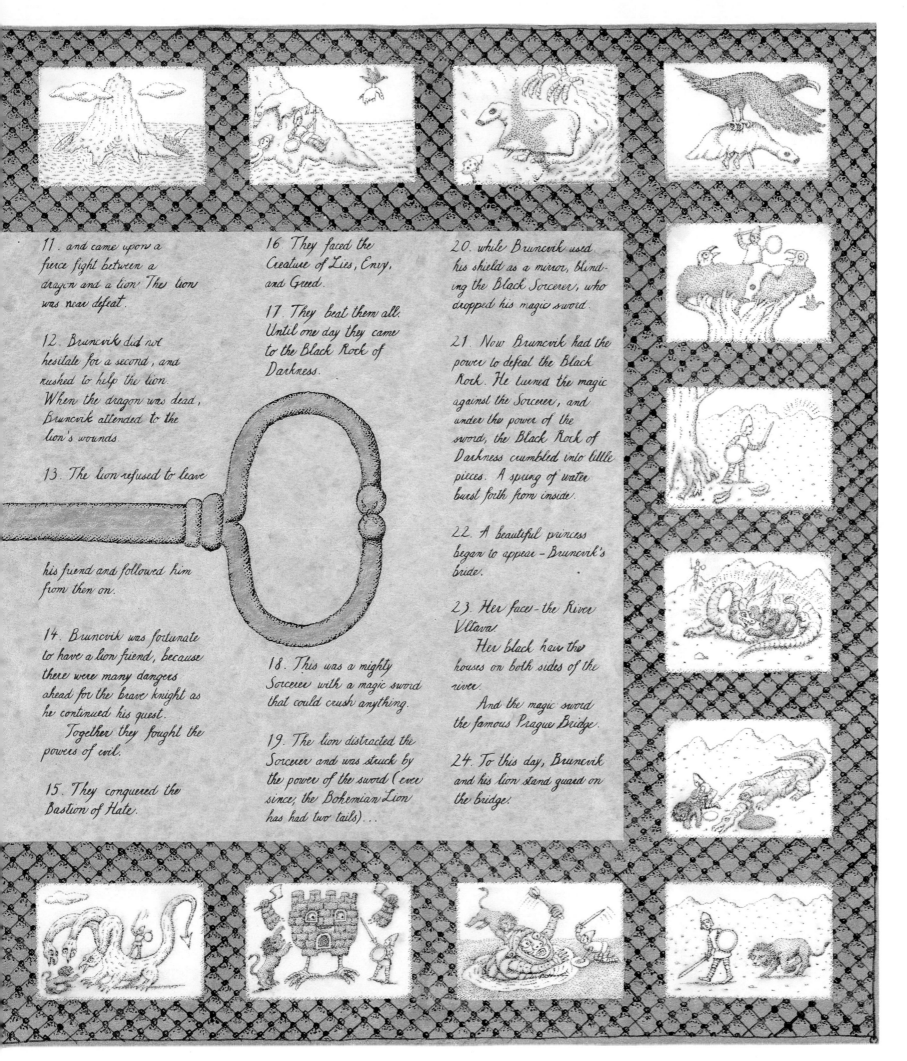

11. and came upon a fierce fight between a dragon and a lion. The lion was near defeat.

12. Bruncvik did not hesitate for a second, and rushed to help the lion. When the dragon was dead, Bruncvik attended to the lion's wounds.

13. The lion refused to leave his friend and followed him from then on.

14. Bruncvik was fortunate to have a lion friend, because there were many dangers ahead for the brave knight as he continued his quest.
    Together they fought the powers of evil.

15. They conquered the Bastion of Hate.

16. They faced the Creature of Lies, Envy, and Greed.

17. They beat them all. Until one day they came to the Black Rock of Darkness.

18. This was a mighty Sorcerer with a magic sword that could crush anything.

19. The lion distracted the Sorcerer and was struck by the power of the sword (ever since, the Bohemian Lion has had two tails)...

20. while Bruncvik used his shield as a mirror, blinding the Black Sorcerer, who dropped his magic sword.

21. Now Bruncvik had the power to defeat the Black Rock. He turned the magic against the Sorcerer, and under the power of the sword, the Black Rock of Darkness crumbled into little pieces. A spring of water burst forth from inside.

22. A beautiful princess began to appear - Bruncvik's bride.

23. Her face - the River Vltava.
    Her black hair the houses on both sides of the river.
    And the magic sword the famous Prague Bridge.

24. To this day, Bruncvik and his lion stand guard on the bridge.

When I finish the story, I am alone, holding the key.

When I stumble
out of the library,
the cat is waiting
to lead me on.
The city seems
different, but still
empty.

Following the cat, I am thinking of those childhood summers in the old town—hide-and-seek, marbles, and the cool air you could feel coming out of the ancient cellars.

Summers in the city. Playing games till late at night. But piano lessons, too.
(Can I hear sounds of music from the open windows?) Slices of fresh baked
bread with ripe tomatoes. The cat is waiting again.

I reach the entrance to a garden. Didn't we come here as boys on one of our expeditions? The cat is hiding in the bushes, whipping her tail.

Then the plants begin to grow and expand. Flowers and fruit. Shapes and forms. The Emperor appears! Everything is deathly silent.

The garden has turned into the Emperor's court! The Emperor himself is opening a scroll with another golden key. He gives it to me . . .

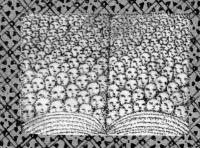

THE GOLEM

In the sixteenth century, under the patronage of the Emperor Rudolph II, Prague became a center for the arts and sciences, as well as for alchemy and the occult. Throughout human history, the myth of the golem – an artificial man – has captivated some of our most creative minds. There are many legends about golems, but the most famous are the ones about the golem created in the sixteenth century by R. Judah Loew ben Bezalel, the Maharal of Prague, to defend the Jews of Prague.

VILLE GLORIEUSE, DOULOUREUSE ET TRAGIQUE
—ANDRÉ GIDE

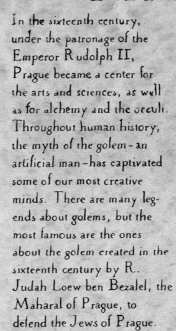

1 For many years, the Ghetto, the Jewish part of Prague, has stood as a complex of crowded dwellings, enclosed by a gated wall.

2. Many, many years ago, there lived a Rabbi Loew, a famous leader of the Jewish community. He was also renowned as a Cabalist – a man with great knowledge of secret magic.

3. Rabbi Loew used to pray and work to improve the desperate conditions in the crowded Ghetto –

4. the suffocating confines, crumbling houses, dreadful disease, gnawing hunger, and almost complete hopelessness.

5. With no other hope in sight, he reached for his magic. From the tears and dreams of his people, he created the Golem.

6. The Golem could project a heart's desires.

He would be seen floating through the dark, narrow streets, giving hope.

7. to the little girl who has never seen butterflies in a green meadow

8. to the devout Jew who has been chased by violent ruffians

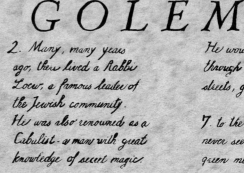

9. to the people who have never felt the warm glow of a fire

10. to the boy who has never seen an abundance of food. But while the Golem could create the illusion, he could not feed the hungry boy...

11. Rabbi Loew realized he had to give the Golem more power.

I read the story on the ancient paper. It is another tale from my childhood.

12. He placed the Shem (a magic stone inscribed with the unutterable name of God) on the forehead of the artificial man.

13. Now the Golem was truly able to help the people. Loew made the Golem brew porridge for everybody in the Ghetto.

14. Everybody came, and everybody was fed.

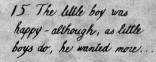

15. The little boy was happy - although, as little boys do, he wanted more...

16. Time went by. The mighty Golem helped around the synagogue.

17. He also helped around the house. And the hungry little boy was always watching out for his opportunity to get more food...

18. Rabbi Loew would remove the Shem from the forehead of the Golem every Friday at sunset, to keep him from working on the Sabbath.

19. Once, however, Rabbi Loew forgot, and when he

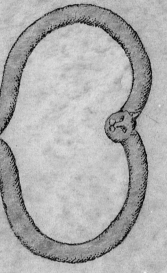

set out for the synagogue to officiate at the Friday evening service,

20. the hungry boy ordered the Golem to brew porridge.

21. But the child did not know how to make the Golem

stop... The porridge rose to the ceiling, and then ran out the door.

22. The sticky flood poured into the temple. Rabbi Loew interrupted the singing of the 92nd Psalm. Had he waited a moment longer, the Sabbath would have begun, and his people would have been trapped.

23. He led his flock to the highest ground in the Ghetto - the cemetery. Even the hungry little boy made it in time.

24. As for the Golem, he was never found. Although people ate porridge for a long time, they could not find him anywhere.

Some say he may still be hiding in the attic of the synagogue...

At the end I am alone with two keys in my hand.

I run to catch up with the cat. The streets seem different again.
Now they remind me of autumn winds . . . the smell of apples, gas-lamp-
lighters with their long tapers, the frozen dew.

We cross the bridge. Still no one anywhere. Memories of flying kites. Disappearing in the fog. Making little people out of chestnuts. Steaming horses pulling the mail carts. Getting up in the dark for school. The cat is rushing ahead.

We arrive at the town square, with its famous clock and with its 27 crosses paved into the sidewalk to commemorate the noblemen executed here a long, long time ago. The door to the clock tower is open. I follow the cat inside.

We find ourselves in a strange dome, filled with a strange collection of things.
Everything is quietly shimmering, motionless, as if frozen in time.

Out of the woodwork come strange mythical robots. The leader, a mechanical baron, brings me another scroll. Here is the third golden key . . . I take it.

HANUS

I BECAME LOST IN THE OPULENT BAROQUE CHURCHES, TRYING TO FIND A NATIVE LAND, ONLY TO LEAVE EMPTIER AND MORE DESPERATE AT THE DISAPPOINTING TÊTE-À-TÊTE WITH MYSELF. I WANDERED ALONG THE VLTAVA CUI INTO SECTIONS BY SEETHING WEIRS. I SPENT ENDLESS HOURS IN THE DESERTED, SILENT HUGE HRADSCHIN DISTRICT.

— ALBERT CAMUS
La mort dans l'âme

Prague's wonderful astronomical clock, or Astrolabium, known locally as *Orloj*, was built by Master Hanus of Růže in 1490. At the time of its construction it could show four time zones at once, along with the present conjunction of the earth, sun and moon in the heavens, the day of the week and month of the year, and also the times the sun would rise and set that day, and the current sign of the zodiac. Every hour on the hour there is an allegorical puppet show with clockwork figures - Vanity, the Grim Reaper, a Miser, and a Turk - while the Twelve Apostles parade past two windows until the cock flaps his wings and crows.

It is said that the clock broke down after Master Hanus's death. In the eighteenth century, the city council was about to dismantle it, but it was saved thanks to the entreaties of a famous astronomer.

1. Many years ago everybody knew of Master Hanus, the renowned clockmaker,

2. inventor, creator of unusual objects,

3. time machines, robots, and androids.

4. He was a man of great knowledge and know-how of all kinds of mechanical magic.

5. No wonder the city elders chose him to create the town clock.

6. The town clock was to be on the face of the proud Town Hall, which towered over the main square.

7. This was a challenge for Master Hanus. He put up scaffolding and designed a clock the likes of which had never been seen before.

8. Although a machine, it was like an ingenious organism, almost a living thing.

I read yet another story from my childhood.

9. It had a clockwork head, eyes, and mouth;

10. sensitive mechanical hands.

11. And for this wondrous creature-like creation...

12. Master Hanus even invented a clockwork carousel, with the Twelve Apostles parading by every hour, on the hour.

13. The long-awaited day of the clock's inauguration finally arrived.

14. Everybody came to see what had never been seen before.

15. And everyone was thrilled beyond expectation. It was the most beautiful clock in the world.

16. A truly magical clock. But certain people started to ask, "What if Master Hanus were to build an even better clock for another city?"

17. Master Hanus was resting after his rewarding work, when

18. masked men crept into his room under the cover of night and blinded him!

19. He was left to bleed to death.

20. For a long time, no one knew what went on behind the darkened windows of Master Hanus's house.

21. Then one night a strange machine rolled out the door. It had fiery eyes and rattled loudly on the cobblestones.

22. It headed toward the clock tower on the old town square.

23. The strange machine with its mechanical eyes disappeared inside the clock tower. Everything grew dark again and there was silence...the clock had stopped.

24. And down from the clock tower those fierce mechanical eyes beamed out over the streets, squares, bridges, and alleys, searching for the men with dark secrets in their minds and for all those people who had watched with silent indifference.

And at the end I am all alone, with all three golden keys in my hand.

With three golden keys in my hand the ancient city seems filled with spring-time—the old town square clock is silently waving good-bye.

The face of the clock smiles and wishes me well. I think of when we children used to wait for the march of the apostles as the clock chimed each hour and the skeleton rang the bell.

I follow the
determined cat
back across the
ancient bridge.
We seem to sail
through the
clouds on the
river. I remember
beautiful springs,
the first fresh
leaves, Easter
eggs, cake in the
shape of a lamb,
the maypole, and
a blue, blue sky.

I feel as though many others just like me have passed here before, and many will be walking forever after, in different times, different ages—like time-travelers caught in one frozen universal second.

And then I am back
in the winding
streets of my
childhood—streets
filled with games,
Sunday family
walks, birthday
cakes, bruised
knees, and the
memory of a day
long ago when
I said good-bye to
this forever.

All those days, months, and years I had tried to recall every stone, every voice, thinking I would never again see them as they used to be. For one fearful moment, I imagine that *no one* is waiting for me.

We are back at the family house. The three golden keys fit into the three
rusty padlocks. The door slowly squeaks open. My cat rushes in.
I open the door wide . . .

I hear my mother's voice : "Peter, wash your hands—it's time for dinner . . ."
I hear voices in the streets. Everything comes alive.

"Madeleine, let's go and wash our hands. Dinner is ready !"

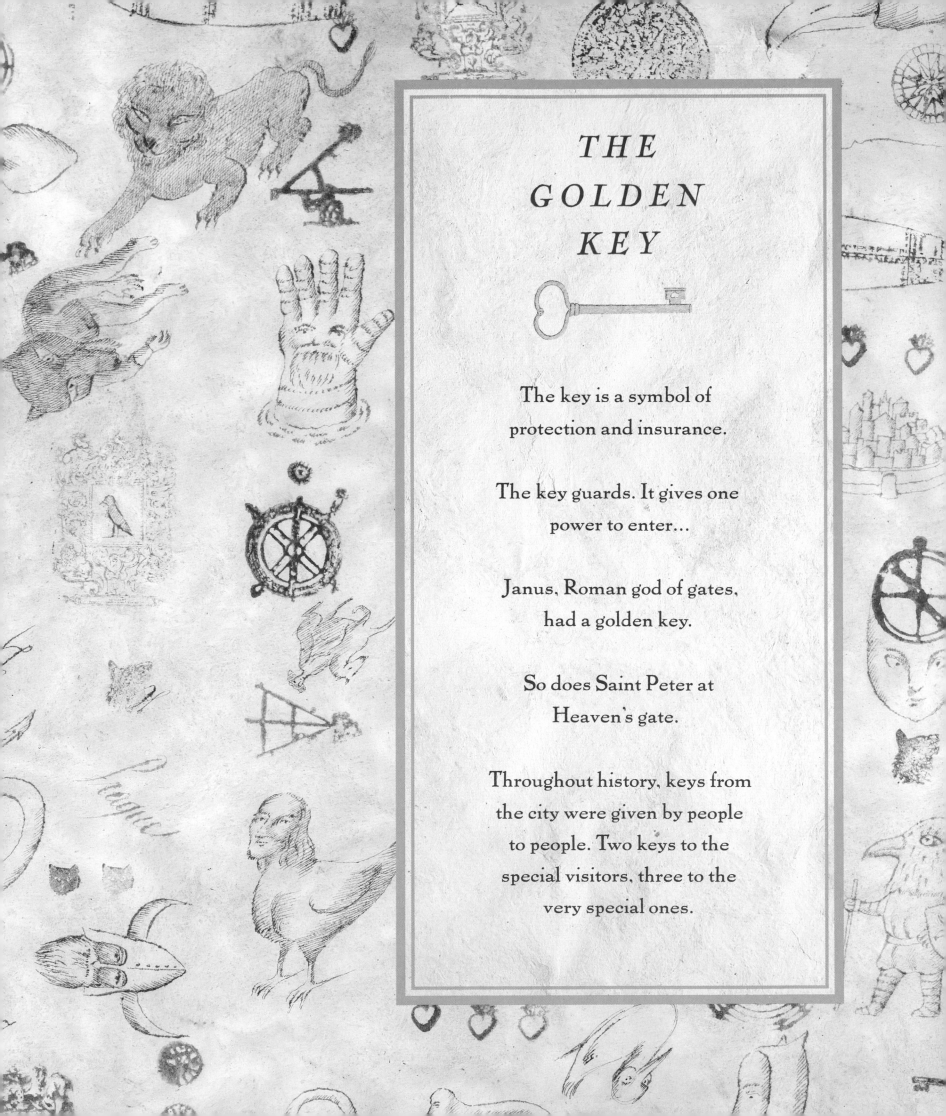

THE GOLDEN KEY

The key is a symbol of
protection and insurance.

The key guards. It gives one
power to enter...

Janus, Roman god of gates,
had a golden key.

So does Saint Peter at
Heaven's gate.

Throughout history, keys from
the city were given by people
to people. Two keys to the
special visitors, three to the
very special ones.